THE
MOON DRAGON

Moira Miller ✎ pictures by Ian Deuchar

Dial Books for Young Readers

New York

Many years ago in China there was a young man named Ling Po.
There was no one more boastful.

He refused to join in when the other boys from the village ran races.

"I can run faster than the wind," he claimed. "I would leave you far behind. But of course I have better things to do with my time."

When the fishermen came home with the biggest catch the village had ever seen, Ling Po laughed.

"That is nothing compared to the fish I caught last year. I had to throw him back or he would have sunk my boat. He made the great wave that you all thought was caused by a storm."

There was no young man more boastful than Ling Po.

Now it happened that the first day of spring was the start of the Kite Flying Festival when the people of Ling Po's village came together to welcome back the sun and the warm winds of summer. They had spent all winter making their beautiful paper kites to carry that welcome high into the clouds.

Ling Po had made no kite of his own, but he laughed at the efforts of the others.

"Call that a butterfly? It looks more like an old crow."

"That will never fly above the cabbage plants, much less soar like an eagle above the treetops. Now if I made a kite, it would be a thousand times stronger, fly higher and farther, and . . ."

"Could it fly to the moon?" asked an old woman who had listened long enough to his boasting.

"Of course," said Ling Po.

"And be so strong that it might even carry a man?"

"Most certainly!" boasted Ling Po. "It would be the finest kite ever seen in China, and I should call it the Moon Dragon."

"Just fancy," said the old woman to her neighbor. "Ling Po says he could build a kite that might fly to the moon and be strong enough to carry a man."

"Amazing!" said the neighbor to the village gossips. "Ling Po is building a kite and he says it might take a man to the moon."

"Incredible!" said the gossips. "Just imagine – Ling Po is determined to fly to the moon."

In no time at all, word of Ling Po's great adventure spread from village to village.

"When will you start building your kite, Ling Po?" asked the baker.

"Soon, soon," said Ling Po. "I am too busy just now, but you will see." He hurried off, hoping they would forget his boast.

But the story spread, as stories will, from village to town, and from town to city. At last it reached the gardens, then the kitchens, then the hall of the Great Imperial Palace. It came to the ear of the Emperor himself.

"This young man is a fine example to us all," said the Emperor. He issued a State Proclamation.

"Be it known that the Great High Emperor of China will graciously attend Ling Po on the occasion of his flight to the moon. From this time forth his name will surely be famed throughout the land."

There was nothing else to be done. Ling Po had to start building the Moon Dragon.

He worked in the shed behind his house. He worked all day.
And all night.

"Ling Po," said the old woman, "your shed is far too small for such a wonderful kite. Let us help you carry it out into the field."

So Ling Po had to build the Moon Dragon in his field, and the villagers all came to watch and to marvel.

"If you are flying to the moon," said the old woman, "you must have a basket to sit in."

"Go away!" hissed Ling Po. But he had to design a basket to hang beneath the Moon Dragon.

He worked very, very slowly.

"When are you going?" asked the villagers.

"Not this year," said Ling Po. "There is still too much to be done." He knew that if he left the Moon Dragon in the field, the winter rains would destroy the fine paper.

"Then we must help you finish it," said the old woman. "Never let it be said that the Great Ling Po – whose name will be famed throughout the land – is lacking in friends."

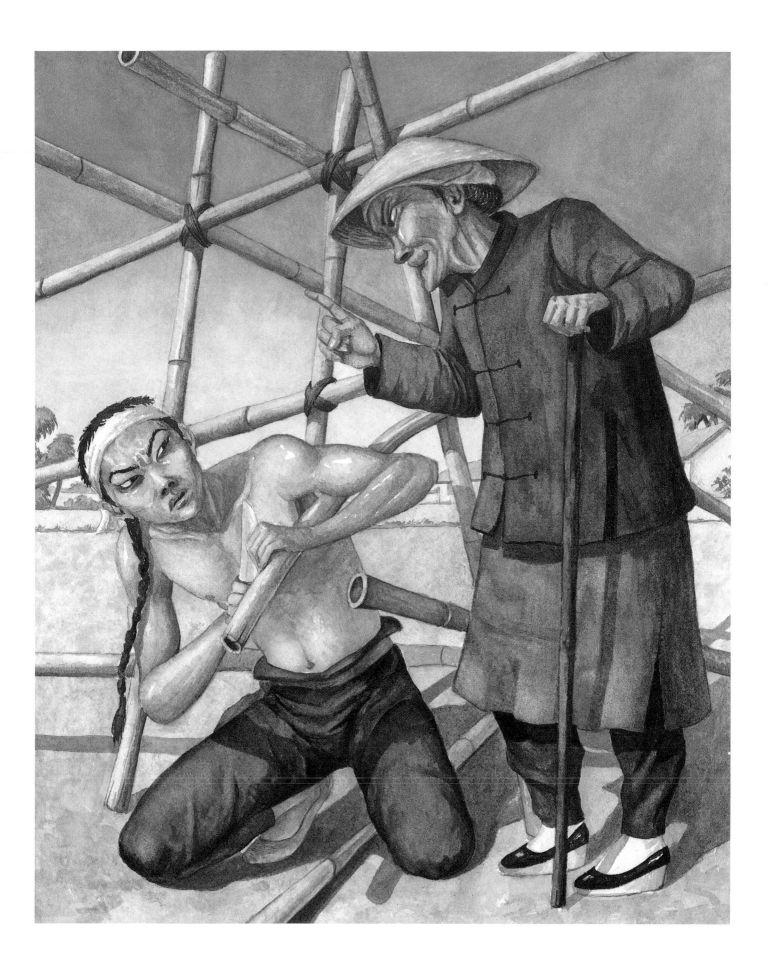

Everyone helped. Some painted, some shaped bamboo poles, some
made ropes. The children of the village helped to finish the basket.
"It is ready to fly," said the old woman to her neighbor.

The neighbor spoke to the gossips, and the gossips spread the word through village and town to the city. It reached the garden, then the kitchen, then the hall of the Great Imperial Palace.

"Ling Po is ready to fly to the moon," said the Emperor.

He came in splendor with all his court: fifty of his bravest knights, a hundred beautiful ladies, and five hundred servants to wait upon them all.

On the night of the full moon they gathered in the field behind Ling Po's house.

"Perhaps it is not quite windy enough," said Ling Po.

"Nonsense," said the old woman. "See how the little clouds hurry across the sky? They have heard that the Moon Dragon is coming and are afraid it will bump into them. Climb into the basket and we will give you food for the journey."

"But there is not enough food in the village for such a journey," said Ling Po.

"Then you must take ours," said the Emperor.

Ling Po had to climb into the basket and the five hundred servants passed in bread and rice, fish, meat, and fruit for the journey. As he was stacking it, the kite suddenly began to rise.

"How brave," said the Emperor. "He cannot wait to set out on his great adventure."

The fifty knights seized the rope and the Moon Dragon lifted high into the sky. The hundred beautiful ladies waved good-bye and the servants and villagers cheered.

Ling Po could see their lanterns disappearing beneath him like tiny stars. He shut his eyes tightly and held onto the basket.

Up and up he soared into the cold night sky. Dragon teeth snapping

at the moon, dragon tail whipping at the clouds.

Over treetops and houses he soared, through clouds and out across the sea.

And still he kept his eyes shut tight.

He landed at last with a gentle bump and the Moon Dragon folded its wings about the basket. Ling Po crawled out. The ground was rocky and dry. There was no moon in the dark sky above his head.

"Can it be true?" he whispered. "Can it really be true?" He stood up slowly, stuck out his chest, and threw his arms wide.

"I, the Mighty Ling Po, have landed on the moon and claim it on behalf of the Great High Emperor of China."

His voice echoed in the darkness. Behind him there came another sound. A tiny giggling, silvery sound.

"Come out and show yourself, moon creature," he roared. "Ling Po, Bravest Man on Earth, will soon teach you to make fun of your betters."

The tiny giggling sound grew to a great gale of laughter as other voices joined in.

Suddenly all around him torches and lanterns lit up the night. Ling Po could see that the Moon Dragon had landed at the other end of his own field.

The Great High Emperor, his fifty brave knights, hundred beautiful ladies, five hundred servants, and all the villagers stood around him, roaring with laughter.

Ling Po raced into his house and hid, but he could still hear them.

The story spread, as stories will, from palace to town, and from town to village until the whole of China knew of the Moon Dragon.

Ling Po became very quiet after that and was never heard to boast again, but his name did become famous throughout the land, just as the Great High Emperor had promised.

From that time on, in cottage or palace, if ever anyone seemed unhappy or worried, a friend only had to whisper "Ling Po" to make him laugh again.

First published in the United States 1989
by Dial Books for Young Readers
A Division of NAL Penguin Inc.
2 Park Avenue
New York, New York 10016

Published in Great Britain by Methuen Children's Books Ltd
Text copyright © 1989 by Moira Miller
Pictures copyright © 1989 by Ian Deuchar
Printed in Belgium
First Edition
(c)
1 3 5 7 9 10 8 6 4 2

Library of Congress Cataloging in Publication Data
Miller, Moira. Moon dragon.
Summary: Ling Po, the most boastful man in all of
China, claims that he can build a kite that will take
him to the moon.
[1. Folklore—China.] I. Deuchar, Ian, ill. II. Title.
PZ8.1.M6174Mo 1989 [398.2] [E] 88-3902
ISBN 0-8037-0566-2